static:

stories

static:

stories

frederick pelzer

etchings press
indianapolis, indiana

This publication is made possible by funding provided by
the College of Arts and Sciences and the English Department
at the University of Indianapolis. Special thanks to IngramSpark and to the
students who judged, designed, and edited this chapbook:
Mikaela Bielawski, Madeline Eash, Rachel Holtzclaw,
Kayleigh Jordan, Jessica Tillman, and Kristen Yates.

UNIVERSITY *of*
INDIANAPOLIS.

Published by Etchings Press
1400 E. Hanna Ave.
Indianapolis, Indiana 46227
All rights reserved

etchings.uindy.edu
www.uindy.edu/cas/english

Printed by IngramSpark
ingramspark.com

Published in the United States of America

ISBN 978-0-9903475-0-7

23 22 21 20 19 18 17 16 15 14   2 3 4
Second Printing, 2019

For Mom and Dad and the love of stories I inherited,
and for Grace.

Table of Contents

Wolf

"Wolf" is the word carved into his bicep. It is also his name. "I got it done in prison," he explains, shouting over the shitty music in the bar, "by my cellmate, a meth dealer saving up for a sex change."

"Sounds like a sitcom," Ellen says.

"Or an A&E reality series," I say. We're so proud of our cleverness these days.

He rolls the shirt sleeve back down. "We still talk," he says. "Carol and I, we send each other postcards in the mail."

He hands us a stack of them from his backpack, from Wichita, from Harrisburg, from Champaign-Urbana. Every single one is signed "Miss you" in pulsing, angular letters.

I wonder if Ellen has ever needed me that much. I wonder what she is wondering.

I hold a postcard from Norfolk with shipping crates floating into the harbor.

I wonder where Carol is now and if she is happy there.

Ad Astra

A tattooed phrase hides under the arch of her foot. "Ad Astra," she says, one finger tracing the ink like a memory. "To the stars." Then her fingers aim up through my ceiling in the shape of a gun and she fires invisible bullets at the night.

She is naked in my bed, but all that I want to look at is this tattoo on the bottom of her foot. "My mission statement at eighteen," she says. Eighteen. Who else has seen this hidden part of her? Who held her hand as the gun pierced her skin? Who else knew that she wanted nothing more than to be gone from this little town?

I kiss her on the bottom of her foot and she giggles, like she must have once when she was eighteen. "Gross," she says. She leans forward to kiss me proper-like. I do not let go of her foot, my fingers against the deadened flesh, squeezing tight. I am going to ask her. Who else was there? Who else knows? Who? Who?

Canvas

///

It was the blank canvas, stretched across the wooden boards until hard with intent, that frightened her. Hanging at the end of the hall. Poorly lit. A centerpiece to the apartment that Emily couldn't understand.

"Why do you keep this thing around?" she asked, the fifth time she'd come to his place, after he'd made her the fancy French meal with birds inside of birds that was far better than she'd ever been prepared to give him credit for. "What's the point?" she asked.

Jon glanced up from the couch, his baby face and tousled hair. Emily was suspicious of him for these very reasons. "A friend told me it means potential," Jon said. He returned his attention to the candles that he was lighting. Emily, over the course of their time together, discovered the candles to be a central tenant of his lovemaking method. Somewhere along the way it was stamped into the underside of his cerebellum that a woman could only truly be pleasured in bed if done in the warmth of candlelight. She worried the day he burned himself alive would happen while she was there.

From his tone and the growing scent of vanilla in the apartment and the way he was staring more at her than at the blank canvas, Emily understood that he didn't have anything else to say about it.

Jon was not given to pieces of art or introspection, his loft in the Strip District sparsely decorated with oversized furniture pressed up against the wall. It was clear that someone had told him the how and where of living successfully without ever demonstrating the specifics. And so in the morning, Emily had only the empty canvas as company.

Often, she touched it as she passed. Emily took a History of Art class in college to satisfy her liberal arts requirements, and always hated the post-modernists. Art as commentary on art. That you could put more emphasis on the idea than on the work, that concept triumphed over commitment. She knew that some ex-girlfriend had given it to Jon but could not find out from him who.

When she moved in, she wanted the canvas thrown out. She suggested starting over with their decoration, both of them, sacrificing her own accumulated sense of personality in order to get rid of the canvas. Jon brushed off the idea. She tried tucking it away in a closet, replacing it with one of her own pieces of art (tiny works by local Pittsburgh artists of the Pacific Ocean, which neither she nor the painters had ever seen save in photographs), then accidentally knocking it from the wall. The canvas survived the assaults. If Jon took notice of the efforts he didn't say. Emily decided to get used to it.

Jon proposed to her at the right type of restaurant with a view of downtown from up on Mount Washington, the ring slipped to her on top of a cupcake with blue vanilla icing (her favorite kind) with no chance of her accidentally eating it, and all of her friends and family appearing from their hiding places. As she took the ring and nodded and said yes for a thousand times, the people she knew and the ones she didn't all applauded her.

And that night, after they'd made love in front of a dozen witnessing candles and Jon had collapsed on the bed in his mighty sprawl, she stalked through the rooms of their apartment. At the end of the hall, where it split towards the living room on one side and the bathroom on the other, waited the canvas. She took it down from the wall and her nails pressed against its whiteness. She held the corner of it to one of Jon's candles until the flame migrated and expanded, greedy, greedy.

Super Fly-Weight

They call me Light-Weight Leonard. But really I'm super light-weight, I'm fly-weight, I'm super fly-weight. I can slip between the elastic bands without touching either. I'm in the ring with Kellen and he eyes me with his one twisted eye but it doesn't do anything to me. I punch my gloves together and duck my feet around.

The bell. He comes on heavy. It's practice, so nobody cares that he's got thirty pounds on me, towers over me in the ring. Nobody cares that I'm taking hits on my arms, my chest, my head. Nobody cares that he's peering at me from the future with his crazy eye or that I hustled to practice early to queue up next to him. And Kellen, all Kellen cares about is I'm a punching bag that can move. I'm a guy he can pound without worrying about it.

But when you're my weight and keep coming back for punishment, you learn a few things. You learn how to slip a knee at the balls without the refs or coaches catching it. You learn how to pack the padding of your gloves without making them too clunky or stiff. You learn how to track down a motherfucker who's seeing your girl behind your back.

Stacy probably called Kellen, let him know what was coming for him in the ring today. But he thinks checking his phone before lacing up is bad luck. He hasn't heard about Stacy in the hospital or the sirens heading our way. He just sees my slim shoulders, and nothing about my oversized fists coming for his head like justice.

You Need To Stop Texting Me

"You need to stop texting me that you want to eat my heart," she says over breakfast, which is just OJ. "It's not as romantic as you think it is."

"Hardly," I say, and I make another notch in the tally on my forearm of the things she doesn't like anymore. The good rule is twenty strikes and you're out.

"You're using up my text limit." She gets up, a tank-top and boyshorts that a boy would never wear, green racing stripes over a gray field. Her hip bones show over the lace, and I worry about her again. I want to grab her as she walks past, kiss her neck and slip my hands down past the lace boundary into southern lands. I don't. Another tally. Seventeen.

"I could say it to your face in the morning," I say.

"Don't," she says. She grabs the black Sharpie from my hand and chucks it in the trash. "Don't be so literal."

While she showers I flip through the pages of my latest inking assignment. There's nothing in the bunch that I want to do. The same oversized muscles bouncing off each other in the name of saving the universe, hiding behind new masks and color schemes and idiotic names. Men and women so disproportionate that steroids must have been involved. My reference models are useless in the face of such Übermensch. I once had a choice in these things.

I'm arranging pens in geometric shapes when she comes out in just a towel. She rushes past into the bedroom and closes the door before getting dressed. I use a 9B pencil to notch another line in my skin. Eighteen.

She leaves without saying another word to me, dressed in a blouse and skirt and shoes like her mother once wore. Nineteen. After she's gone, I take out the dish soap and scrub away the marks so we are once more at zero.

Ghost

//

The ghost has been haunting the kitchen for days. Greg likes to throw things at her. I just try to ignore her. She uses her time productively, cutting and cleaning and generally trying to help, only her hands sometimes go through objects. This frightens her each time, and I just want to save her.

She was there when we first moved in, and I can only guess she still will be when we leave. The rest of the time she likes to hide.

I sit with Greg in the living room, *Pride and Prejudice* in my lap. I hate Jane Austen, but the book club has forced it us and there's no fighting that. Well, I'm not fighting it. Greg has enacted his own tiny uprising against the book club, refusing to read the book. It's really counterproductive. He still comes to the meetings and tries to contribute to the conversation even though he doesn't know what's going on.

"I always find Mr. Darcy so romantic," Priscilla says. She's the one who suggested that our next book be *Pride and Prejudice* and has proudly told us that she reads it every year. "This is the way relationships are supposed to happen," she says.

"What do you think he smells like?" Greg asks. "Is it like wild grass or a woman's perfume?" He's earnest when he asks these questions, thinks that he's helping, but really. The others stare at him. I laugh into my hand, which I then smell, and it does not smell like a woman's perfume.

"Please excuse Greg," I say.

"I don't need excusing," he says.

"Where have all the Mr. Darcys gone?" Priscilla asks. No one else in the book group has an answer. The book is heavy on my lap.

I like to watch the ghost work. There is something soothing in her slow motions, her gentle ways. Greg comes home from the office and starts shouting at her. "Get the fuck out of here!" he says. "This is no longer your home!"

"We don't know what she wants," I say.

"It wants an easy ride," he says. "To hell with that."

"Maybe she's just lonely," I say.

Greg goes to the living room and puts on the World Series of Poker. He watches for the rest of the night, growling at the screen like a stray mutt. I make dinner side by side with the ghost, who attempts to make a sandwich, again and again. The bread and meat are there, but she just cannot get a grip on the cheese. Right as I take the dense meatloaf out to join Greg, I place the cheese for her. She does not look at me, just takes the plate and sinks through the floor. But she must have forgotten that the plate is not like her, because it gets left behind on the kitchen floorboards. It is pastrami and mozzarella, my favorite. I eat it quickly before Greg can see.

"Why the hell would you fold that?" Greg shouts at the screen. He's part of a poker fantasy league with the other guys from his office. It's a pretty big deal for them. This year he asked me for two hundred dollars to put into the pot. We don't have two hundred dollars but I gave it to him anyway. The television shows the hand of another player, clubs and spades, and Greg grabs a chunk of the meatloaf and throws it at the screen. It splatters all over, blending in with the tiny dots of light to create a new image of a man in sunglasses with a meatloaf-esque birthmark on his cheek. It does not seem that we will be getting the two hundred back.

"You should get a divorce." My mother. Greg is the last link in a chain of boyfriends she didn't like. "It's not right, the way he treats that poor woman." My mother met the ghost the year before, during Thanksgiving, and they became close friends, spending long hours together in the basement. Through the cracked wooden door and down the creaking steps leading to the shadowy pit of the basement, I could hear them laughing. I wished that I could join them down there, but the door remained closed. When my mother returned to the kitchen, she wiped the tears from her eyes. "Why couldn't you have been a lesbian?" she asked me, and I put down the crackers I was eating and shrugged.

"I love Greg very much," I tell her now. I'm lying on our bed upstairs. It's weird to think of a master bedroom as a thing you live in. Master bedrooms should only ever hold your parents. "We are very happy."

"That woman isn't." My mother sighs. She is a world class sigher, my mother. Her sighs carry heft. They are strong enough to knock my father over, and he looks like a circus strongman in his leopard print. "It breaks my heart what he does."

"What about me?" I say. "Don't you care about what he does to me?"

"I thought you said you were happy?" she says.

"That's what he does to me," I say.

At night I like to sit with the ghost on the back porch while I smoke. Greg doesn't know I've kept the habit up. The ghost is very quiet during these times. Sometimes she looks at me like she wants a cigarette, but I'm not going to give it to her until she asks for it.

When we first moved in, the realtor said the ghost was a big draw. "Great conversation starter," she told us. "Constant entertainment. And you'll never have rats!" It was true about the rats though.

Inside the house is my copy of *Pride and Prejudice*. I've decided I'm not going to finish it. I can't stand Mr. Darcy. If I were Elizabeth I would not have wasted the time on such a wall of a man. Since I'm not reading it, there really is no point in going to the meetings either, at least for a little while.

The ghost's stare wears me down. I pass her a cigarette. She places it in her translucent mouth and I light the tip for her. In these quiet moments she has an easy grace. They found her body in the basement of the house, torn apart by her husband, blood everywhere. The realtor could say what she wanted about the benefits, but we still got a good price on the place.

Also inside is Greg, going over our money situation. He will be stressed and drinking too much coffee. His ulcer will be bothering him. His wire-frame glasses will glint in the electric light, hiding his eyes.

The cigarette passes through the ghost's lower lip, slides down into her chest, and settles upon the steps within her. I entertain the thought of being like her. Nothing sticks. Everything passes through.

Already A Regret

//

She had a tattoo, sure, but she liked to cover it up with high-collar shirts. I didn't even find out about it until our sixth date. We were already on our way towards ending the relationship—not a break-up since there wasn't anything really worth breaking up. But when I stopped in at her place and came into the bathroom I thought was empty, I saw the words curling around the back of her neck: "Set yourself on fire." She slapped her hand across them. "Get out," she said, and I did.

We were friends after, the first time I ever managed the landing of a relationship. We met for coffee outdoors, and I said, "I don't think this is working," and she said, "I was going to say something next week." We hugged, and I thought just maybe I was growing up some.

And so later, at the wedding, I figured she was the only woman in my life I could call a friend, not just an ex- or an almost- or about-to-be- or want-to-be-girlfriend. During the rehearsal dinner I asked her what was wrong with me.

"Nothing," she said. We were out on the back patio of the restaurant, and she was having the last cigarette of her life. The smoke reminded me of the forest and would inspire me to start smoking again the next night, during the reception, after which I would sleep with her maid-of-honor and finally convince her to stop talking to me.

"You just think you believe in true love."

I saw that the tattoo was gone from her neck, removed in preparation for the wedding and its endless photos, no doubt. A slim scar stood in its place. I wondered if the guy she was marrying even knew that she'd once branded herself with an untenable life goal.

I asked her for the rest of her pack of cigarettes, but she shook her head no and patted me on the cheek. We were both already starting to think that maybe me being at the wedding was a bad idea. She went back inside. I remained.

Static

Here's a story: Ana had dated a lot of assholes and I'd been one of them. One night in New York City she passed a store front where they had a stack of televisions playing different channels and she stopped to watch the news happening on one of the screens, in the far bottom right corner of the pyramid of broadcasting. It was winter in New York City just like in the movies and it was snowing and she was wearing a pink knit cap long before they came back into fashion.

On this newscast there came a report about a fire, a terrible fire in the Bronx, an apartment building gone and a family consumed, mother, son, son, and daughter. Ana couldn't hear what they were saying but the headlines confirmed all the worst possible suspicions. And Ana said, of course, of course, New York, you know how to treat me. Because Ana had just dumped another of those assholes who had come after me and matched the assholes before me, a chain of mirrors around me.

And when she got home Ana called me up and she said hello asshole and I said hi Ana and she said here's a story and told me about the fire.

You know what I've been thinking she said.

No of course not I said.

She said:

I've been thinking this is a pretty terrible place.

She said:

I've been thinking about getting out of here.

She said:

I think I'm through with New York. I think New York and me are broken up.

I asked if she'd been drinking and she said of course she had why else would she be calling me and it was true. I'd drunkenly called her once in college and told her I was in love with someone else while she was sober and ever since she thought she had the right to drunk dial me and leave long wobbling messages on my answering machine. And I don't know she's wrong to do so. I keep telling her what my new number is.

Where would you go? I asked. I couldn't imagine a New York without Ana, or vice versa, even though I hadn't seen her in person in ten years.

Anywhere else she said.

I hear that Antarctica is very nice this time of year she said.

Of course it is I said.

The thing of it is is that me and New York are in an abusive relationship Ana said. New York keeps throwing these terrible men at me and I keep smiling and coming back for more.

That does sound like a serious issue I said. I wasn't doing my best in this conversation, because on my end of the line the woman I'd met ten years too late / right on time, the woman I'd once drunkenly told Ana I was in love with instead of her, was kissing my neck. This time I wisely chose to withhold the information.

Maybe I'm a lesbian Ana said, which meant she'd

been drinking sangria. To which I said of course not and this was probably true.

Maybe I'm secretly asexual Ana said.

The woman on my end of the phone was very definitely being the opposite of asexual and I wasn't brave enough to stop her. That doesn't sound right either I said with a tiny bit of quiver in my voice.

I guess I'm doomed Ana said. I grunted in response.

Maybe I should come over there Ana said and suddenly there was a great deal of energy in her voice, all of it coming down in the word *there*, like the energy of the idea alone would teleport her from Brooklyn to Manhattan.

Maybe not I said. But there was no one on the other end having a conversation with me. I was dialoguing with the static.

I told the woman I'd met ten years too late / right on time I'd be back in a second, pulled on a shirt, jogged down the eight flights to the ground floor of my building and burst out into the same snow which earlier fell on Ana while she stared at the bottom right television. All snow in New York is the same snow, recycled until it turns white again. That snow never escapes the city.

Of course she wouldn't be there instantly. She'd just hung up the phone. The odds were good she wouldn't even come, just crawl into bed after getting me antsy by saying she was coming over.

I looked up the street, then down it. In the night in the snow I didn't see anyone like her, tall and curved like a dew drop, and it was cold and colder and I was in slippers so I gave it up for a bad game. As the door rattled shut behind me I heard knocking. There was Ana, waving at me, all done up in warm winter clothes.

I came back outside.

What are you doing here? I asked. How'd you get here so fast?

There's a woman upstairs isn't there Ana said.

And so what if there is I said.

I can smell it in your blood she said. All men's blood smells the same when there's a woman upstairs.

I pictured my red blood on top of the white snow.

What do you want Ana? I asked.

Come drink with me she said.

No I said. That was ten years ago and someplace else. I'm the asshole you drunk dial and tell stories to. There is a woman upstairs. I'm not getting a drink with you.

If you don't I'll kill myself she said.

I'm sorry she said.

That wasn't funny she said.

No it wasn't I said.

We both looked down at the fallen snow.

You want to hear a story? she asked.

Not really I said.

She returned to Brooklyn and continued to date assholes. Something about her guarantees it. I never told Ana that it was the woman from ten years ago upstairs.

Here's a story: my mother died. She died like a coward, which is why I know I will live like a coward. She jumped in front of the LIRR, on a crowded platform, while a hundred people watched. Plus me.

I told Ana about it back when we were dating.

That's fucked up she said.

I know I said.

Why would you tell me that? she said.

Because we're bonding I said, desperate for it to be true. I was already a little bit in love with the woman upstairs, right there in college, but she had a boyfriend and plans that didn't involve me and I knew it. Ana and I lay on top of my standard issue single bed in my dorm room. I was a senior but also an RA and in charge of the honors floor for some reason. Ana lived off campus and liked to come slumming around the little freshmen with her musical tattoos scribed across her shoulders, walking mostly naked to the showers in the morning.

I guess I should tell you a story too Ana said. I told her it seemed fair. I hadn't admitted yet I loved the woman upstairs, not to Ana and not to myself. That would come later.

Here's a story Ana said. It takes place on the Pennsylvania farm where I grew up, south of here. The land bleeds away into West Virginia where all the cows have ingrown teeth, just like their owners.

They do not I said.

This is my story Ana said. Where was I?

Cows with ingrown teeth I said.

Right she said. The dogs are like that too. But that's West Virginia. On my farm we've got normal dogs, because it's Pennsylvania. And it's no longer a farm. It was once, but by the time we moved out there, a bunch of Cubans fleeing Castro as fast as we could, it was no more. My parents made it as far as Bobtown and could go no further, so they buried their Spanish and raised us like we belonged here.

Since it was once a farm, there's a farmhouse and a barn. One night my brother and I went down to the barn. He was six. I was ten. I made fun of him for being afraid, but I was afraid too. The clouds covered up the moon and my fear. The only light was the flashlight I had.

You see, in the barn was the ghost of my grandfather. He followed us from Cuba where he'd vanished into Castro's secret prisons. Mi abuelo. He lived in the barn. My parents talked about him all the time. My brother and I weren't allowed to go inside. But we were children, so we were brave, and we went inside.

What did you see I asked.

Nothing she said. No one was there. Ghosts aren't real. What's past is past. This is just a story. Don't be stupid.

The last story I told to Ana was about the woman upstairs. I called Ana from my dorm room while I was drunk and she was sober, it's true. One day earlier Ana and I had been making plans for the apartment we would move into together after graduation, and now the first words out of my slurring mouth were:

Here is a story.

Here is a story I said. I'm in love and it's not with you.

I explained how I knew, sitting in the Hillman Library on the fifth floor studying for a final with the woman upstairs, just the two of us, finals week and the place is ours alone. We were preparing for the last final, the Saturday final, the one not even the professor wants to show up for. Outside was cold, the snow whipping by sideways in front of the window, but we were warm and dry. We listened to "Out of Time" again and again with the headphones lying on the table between us, turned as loud as possible. We talked about I don't know what.

While I was telling this story Ana said nothing. And eventually I realized she wasn't on the other end, she'd hung up. She'd hung up a while ago and I was just dialoguing with static.

Acknowledgments

Starting at the beginning, due credit to my family for raising me with a love of words. Thanks to the many teachers who helped me along the way, especially Jeff Fluharty for first putting that pen in my hands, and my fantastic teachers at Pitt, who showed me how you tell a story, one word at a time: Karl Hendricks, Jeff Martin, Geeta Kothari, Stephen Coleman, and Kathleen George. Thank you to the many who looked at and gave feedback for the stories in this collection, including members of The Matt McArdle Memorial Workshop Group, The Electric Boogaloo Workshop Group, The Chicago Writers Salon, and every other group who took me in and listened to my words. To the friends who gave me something to do besides write, without you I would have never been able to put down a single word. To *Stymie*, *Flywheel*, and *Microstory*, thank you for printing these words and granting me the confidence to keep going. To the talented students and teachers of Etchings Press who put together this book that you now hold in your hands, I cannot thank you enough. To you, the reader, for picking up a set of stories you've never heard of.

And finally, to Grace, always.

Biography

A graduate of the University of Pittsburgh,
Fred Pelzer lives in Chicago, where he is a
founding member of Cloud Gate Productions.
This is his first book.

Colophon

Cover font in Hoefler Text.
Title font in Gill Sans MT.
Body text in Chaparral Pro.

Etchings Press Chapbook Contest

Etchings Press is a student-run publisher at the University of Indianapolis. Each year, student editors choose the Whirling Prize, a post-publication award, in the fall and coordinate a publication contest for one poetry chapbook, one prose chapbook, and one novella in the spring. For more information, please visit etchings.uindy.edu.

Previous winners and publications

Poetry
2019: *As Lovers Always Do* by Marne Wilson
2018: *In the Herald of Improbable Misfortunes* by Robert
          Campbell
2017: *Uncle Harold's Maxwell House Haggadah* by Danny Caine
2016: *Some Animals* by Kelli Allen
2015: *Velocity of Slugs* by Joey Connelly
2014: *Action at a Distance* by Christopher Petruccelli

Prose
2019: *Dissenting Opinion from the Committee for the Beatitudes*
          by Marc J. Sheehan (fiction)
2018: *The Forsaken* by Chad V. Broughman (fiction)
2017: *Unravelings* by Sarah Cheshire (memoir)
2016: *Pathetic* by Shannon McLeod (essays)
2015: *Ologies* by Chelsea Biondolillo (essays)
2014: *Static: Stories* by Frederick Pelzer (fiction)

Novella
2019: *Savonne, Not Vonny* by Robin Lee Lovelace
2018: *Edge of the Known Bus Line* by James R. Gapinski
2017: *The Denialist's Almanac of American Plague and Pestilence*
          by Christopher Mohar
2016: *Followers* by Adam Fleming Petty

www.ingramcontent.com/pod-product-compliance
Lightning Source LLC
Chambersburg PA
CBHW070318120726
47910CB00007B/2532